T0065228

The Portrait and the Doll

MICHAEL B. CARTWRIGHT

Archway Publishing books may be ordered
through booksellers or by contacting:

Archway Publishing
1663 Liberty Drive
Bloomington, IN 47403
www.archwaypublishing.com
844-669-3957

ISBN: 978-1-6657-5282-4 (sc)
ISBN: 978-1-6657-5283-1 (e)

Library of Congress Control Number: 2023921446

Print information available on the last page.

Archway Publishing rev. date: 11/07/2023

Synopsis

The story is about a young man from the city, who just inherited an aunt's estate, an aunt he does not remember. He traveled to the small town where she lived. He met an antiques dealer in whose shop he discovered a painting of an 19th century young woman holding a doll. The background of the painting he recognized as being in the mansion he just inherited. He bought the portrait. Before he left the shop he spotted the doll in a corner, the doll from the picture you. He bought them both. That is when the nightmare began. The house is haunted by the spirit of A young lady who uses the doll as a means of performing physical acts in the house. The ghost also haunts those who dare reside in the mansion for any period of time. The man who, at first does not believe in the supernatural soon seeks help to put an end to the torment he is being subject to. Mr. Cushing, the shop owner is also an audio medium suggests he see the local historian, who was the sister of the deceased husband of his aunt and also, the historian senses spirit vibrations and can feel what the spirits feel. Her name is Henrietta Lee. In time, miss Lee assembles two others. Mrs. Belasko Who is a channeler and Mr. Pratt who is a visual medium. Together they set about their daunting task to rid the mansion of the malevolent spirit and break the family curse that has plagued the male members of the Carmichael family. Their work, to accomplish this takes them to newspaper archives, the cemetery, the family crypt and the mansion itself. The story, about a vengeful ghost and malevolent doll, is over 19399 words.

I live in the town of Grieg wright. It is a small village located in the upper northeast of the country, on the East Coast. In all, you could not find a more beautiful and tranquil place to live. It has a population of twelve hundred and twenty. Not very notable in a world full of people. There is a wide Main St. With oak trees on both sides that provide cool breezes in the summer and offer some protection to the small shops on the left side of the street in the winter. On the right side lies the ocean, about fifty yards past the trees.

Traveling down the five miles of Main Street are two corners on the left. The first corner one comes to leads out of town to the next "Big City", about 50 miles away. The second corner is much shorter. It is approximately a quarter of a mile with small shops on either side of the street. This section seems to be in perpetual shade. At the end is a Col de sac where one can turn around and go back to Main Street. It is this section of town where my tale begins.

I seldom visit this area but, on this day, I needed to reacquaint myself with the antique/resale shop to see what I could find to complete the decor for the bedroom on the second floor of my ancient home. The house is a large

Victorian, I acquired it upon the death of my aunt. It had been in the family for generations. I had just moved in a few months ago. I never knew my aunt but, for some reason she left me the house in her will.

I parked the car in front of a shabby looking storefront, whose painted sign announced to any would be customer its purpose for being there. As I turned the knob and opened the door, the tinkling of the overhead bell connected to the top of the door, gave out its cheerful alert to the proprietor, that there is a perspective sale to be had. I slowly made my way around the shop, which seemed larger on the inside than it appeared to be on the outside. The place was clean and very orderly. All the items for sale were categorized in two separate sections of the shop for the convenience of the customer. From the curtained backroom emerged the owner of the shop. A tall thin man. He had a narrow face with sunken cheeks leading to a somewhat vee shaped chin he wore wirerimmed glasses, had on a brimmed cap, the type you see men wearing in photographs of the nineteen twenties and a cardigan sweater.

As I browsed the shop, my eyes darted this way and that, the owner came up to me. In a pleasantly soft-spoken cultured voice, he introduced himself as Mister Cushing the proprietor and asked if he could be of assistance in my quest. I explained that I had recently come into possession of the large house on the hill, just outside of town and needed a few items for the bedroom. With the wave of his hand, he pointed and said the "furniture section is that way I am sure you will find exactly what you are looking for Mr.?" -----" Oh, I am sorry the name is Carmichael----Frederick

Carmichael." "Nice to meet you Mr. Carmichael," replied Cushing. With another wave of his hand, he bid me to begin my search.

As I made my way slowly, through a small archway into the next room, I began to look around. As I walked around the room glancing from one item to the next, my eyes fell upon the portrait of a beautiful young woman. She was dressed in a pink satin gown. The type of which was the fashion in the eighteen-sixties high society. On her head rested a matching wide brim hat of satin, placed slightly to the left. She was holding a doll, dressed identical to what she was wearing. I noticed something peculiar. Although I did not recognize the figure in the painting, I seem to recognize the background where the picture was painted. The portrait, being two feet by three feet gave ample identity to the items and wall behind her. I called out for Mister Cushing. He slowly walked my way." Mr. Cushing do you know the history of this painting?" "Well," said he." let us walk over to the counter and go through the auction receipt Ledger." His Bony fingers, thumbing through the pages, suddenly stopped." Ah yes, here it is. It seems that someone from the mansion, the very estate that you own right now brought in a few items from the Misses Carmichael-Lee estate." "Yes," I replied." Lee was my aunt's married name but, I wonder why she would have someone put this up for auction?" "Oh," Cushing stated." He did not want to wait for an auction to take place. He wanted a quick sale. He seemed awfully anxious to be rid of the items. "Well, here is something." After a short pause, I asked, "What would that be?" "It seems the doll in the portrait was sold to me. I almost forgot about that." "What were the other items sold?" I asked. "The doll and the picture were the only things sold to me." Mister Cushing thought for a moment. "Now I remember, the person, I think the butler, seemed to indicate, with extreme nervousness, that a quick sale was imperative. He informed me he quit working for the estate and this was his final duty before heading west. He was glad to be rid of these cursed things." "What did he mean by that?" I inquired. "I do not know, when I asked him, his face turned pale. He accepted the agreed upon price and hurriedly left. Sir, are you interested in purchasing one or perhaps both of these pieces?" "Yes, I think will take both," I replied. After filling out the necessary paperwork and having a feeling of great satisfaction I walked towards the door.

Leaving the shop with my purchases, I put them in my red newer model SUV. I slowly made my way back to the house on the hill. While driving, I was deep in thought about why just these things from the house were sold and nothing else. They should not have sold anything from the estate without my consent unless, my aunt ordered it before her death.

My aunt had lived in her huge mansion alone, after her husband died a few months before. There were only three household staff members. The butler, cook and maid, each had been employed by my aunt for less than three years. Shortly after my aunt's death, all three gave notice and left. No one ever knew why. My aunt dying one day, the servants leaving the next, with no explanation for anyone.

After I arrived back at the mansion and brought the portrait and the doll into the house, I walked into the library and sat them on the floor. It's a room just a short distance from the front door. It is a large room. Walls were of oak paneling, with a polished wooden floor. In the middle of the back wall was a good-sized fireplace, on top of which was a mantle. Sitting on the mantle were pictures and keepsakes of previous owners, I presumed. A photo stood out from the rest; was displayed prominently in the middle, away from the others. It was of a rugged looking man wearing seafaring garb. Partially covering the floor was a huge oriental carpet, on top of which sat a long table surrounded by six dining room chairs. There were two overstuffed leather chairs at the far end of the room and a sideboard against the wall. I walked over to it and poured myself a brandy. I went over and sat down in one of the leather chairs, lit a cigarette and continued to think why these objects and nothing else were sold. I put out the cigarette, finished my drink and went upstairs to bed.

In the morning I awoke, bathed, dressed and came downstairs to fix my breakfast. The kitchen is a large room with all the current essentials a kitchen should have. I decided to eat in the kitchen. I sat down with my usual, cereal, toast and juice, facing the window above the sink. It was a beautiful morning, with the leaves of the large oak trees gently fluttering in the mild breeze while unseen birds were chirping in the distance. The mood was anything but sinister. As I was eating, I suddenly heard a clickety clickety clickety. The sound reminded me of what a mouse might make that was scurrying across a polished wooden floor. I got up from the table, went through the door and into the library. I looked around the room, found nothing out of the ordinary. No sign of a mouse. No droppings or anything else that could be the cause of the strange sounds I heard. I looked over towards the doll and the portrait. I was shocked and astonished. The doll, which I distinctly remember setting on the left side of the picture, was now on its right but, what really froze the blood in my veins was the portrait of the young woman. Her clothes were torn. The left side of her gown was torn, ripped to the waist, hat missing, hair mussed, and the lower half of her gown was disheveled. She was teary eyed but had a vengeful look in her eyes. I could not believe what I was seeing. I rubbed my eyes, closed them and turned away. After a second or two I turned around and the picture was normal again. Needless to say, I was shaken up and could not comprehend what had just occurred. I walked through the library, past the dining room and into the living room, trying to recover from the shock I had just received. I then realized that this was the very room that the portrait had been painted in. The same wall, the same decorations in the background.

Later, in the early afternoon I decided to go back to the antique shop to talk to Cushing. As I parked in front of the shop, I exited the car, stepped onto the sidewalk and turned the knob of the door and walked in, Mister Cushing was there to greet me. "Mister Cushing, I need to talk to you." "Please sir, call me Chris," said he. "Are you sure you do not know anything about the doll and the picture I bought?" "Well sir, like I said it was a quick sale without any haggling about price. We completed the transaction and out he flew," replied Chris. "Well, thank you very much Mister Cushing -----I mean Chris." As I turned to leave, he stated.

"There is one thing you might do to learn more about the house. We have a woman in town who works for the local historical society, she may be able to help you. Go back to Main Street, turn left and the building is on the right side with a small plaque in front." I replied with grateful thanks and left. I got into my car, made the turnaround and drove to meet the woman who might be able to help me. Slowly, driving down the road, my neck craning and eyes straining to find the place, I at last reached my destination. I parked in front of a two-story structure. It was a typical house made of wood, painted white, with black shutters on the two front first floor windows, each located on either side of the front door. I made my way to the door, opened it and walked in." Good afternoon Mr. Carmichael, may I call you Fred?" inquired this person whom I have never met. She must have noticed my startled expression and explained." Oh, I am sorry, Chris just phoned me and said you were on your way here to find out about the Carmichael -Lee house." "Yes, and yes, that is why I am here and yes you may call me Fred," I replied. After shaking hands, she introduced herself as Henrietta Lee, the sister of my late aunt's husband. She asked me to follow her, we stopped at a long wooden table made of oak. There were two chairs standing beside each other. On top of the table sat a heavy volume. Printed on the cover were the years eighteen-fifty-nine to eight-teen sixty-five.

As we sat down, she began to open the volume and search for the information we were seeking. "After Chris called," she said. "I searched until I found what I think might give us some information on what we are looking for."

As she was intently searching through the historical log, pages at a time, she suddenly stopped." Here it is!" She exclaimed." This is it. The house was built in eighteen-sixty. It is a two-story mansion with a circular drive. The inside decor and furnishings were of the finest quality, with no expense spared, the pride of Griegwright." There she paused. "Is that it?" I questioned." Oh no" she continued." The house was built by a retired sea captain named Bartholomew Carmichael. He had three children, Robert, Emily and Pamela." She stopped reading." That is all there is about the house. It continues on about other historical facts of the town," she said." Did your late brother ever mention anything about the house to you?" I questioned." Not really. He always seemed so nervous and agitated though. Whenever I asked him what was wrong, he always said nothing and that I was imagining things. The last few years he became a total recluse, as did your aunt," she replied. As I was about to stand up and leave, Henrietta put her hand on my arm. I sat back down.

"Fred" she said." If you are interested in local folklore and legend about the family, I can tell you the story that everyone around here knows." "Yes, please do." I answered anxiously." Well,", she began." As we discovered, Bartholomew had three children. The oldest was Robert. He was a no good. A bully, drunkard and a womanizer, who brutally treated women with contempt and loathing. Not at all like his father, who was kind, gentle and respectful to everyone." She paused for a moment, then continued." The captain had a second child, his eldest daughter was Emily. She grew into such a lady, a sweet person. The creme of

Griegwright society. Impeccably dressed in the latest fashion from abroad. She was kind to everyone she met, whether they were in her class or plain working people. Everyone adored her. Then there was Pamela. A child six years of age, who by all accounts was a little darling." "Robert associated with Griegwrights most undesirable delinquents. The small group that Robert surrounded himself with came from families of money and of poverty. Most every night could find them drinking at the saloon, harassing the customers, making obscene remarks and gestures to the barmaids. After drinking their fill, they would leave and find what mischief they could create. On this particular night, Robert came home drunk as usual. He was in a foul mood. The hour was late, with the family asleep upstairs except for Emily. She was in the library reading, waiting to admonish him for his deplorable behavior and for tarnishing the family name. He staggered into the library and poured himself a drink." There, Henrietta stopped her narrative and asked if I would like some tea. I respectively decline the offer and urged her to continue." As I said, so the story goes, Emily started to warn him that his behavior could not be tolerated any longer, that after she talked to their father in the morning, she would make him see that something needed to be done to curb Roberts evil ways. Robert just stared at her drink in hand weaving back and forth trying to steady himself, not saying a word, he laughed at Emily and lunged at her. Throwing his drink away he hit Emily with two heavy blows to the face with his rock-like fists, she fell to the floor, unconscious. Not thinking clearly and in a rage, he tore at her dress. He ripped her garment from the shoulder to the waist, then savagely began to remove all her undergarments that ladies of period wore. He slumped to his knees unbuttoned his pants then had his way with her." Henrietta stopped again; her face slightly a washed from embarrassment." Are you sure you would not like a cup of tea or coffee?" she asked again.

Seeing that she needed a break from telling the story, I graciously accepted the offer of a cup of coffee. While she left to prepare the refreshments, I walked through part of the museum, looking around at all old photographs and documents. Some hung on walls, others were displayed on tables. This did not interest me at all, and I waited patiently for miss Lee's return.

"Here we are!" she exclaimed, as she entered the room carrying a small tray with two cups of coffee and some cookies. She sat the tray at the end of the long table we had been sitting at. In front of me she served my coffee in a cup on a matching saucer and put a plate of cookies on the table. She then sat down with her little snack." Please, Henrietta. Is there more?" I asked." Oh, my yes," said she." After the incident, he stumbled up to his room on the second floor and passed out on the bed. A few minutes later, Emily regained consciousness. She, in a daze, gathered up her undergarments and slowly, made her way up the two flights of stairs to her room.""" Then what happened?" I inquired." She sat on her bed, then her personal maid entered the room. She was awakened by a noise outside of her door. You see, her room was next to Emily's in case her mistress may need her." Miss Lee paused for a sip of coffee and a bite of cookie.

"The maid found Emily sitting on the edge of her bed

in a state of disarray, clutching her clothes and eyes staring forward, she not saying a word. The maid gently knelt down in front of her and asked what happened. Emily just kept staring. The maid rose to inform her father, but Emily's hand quickly rose and grabbed her arm. She finally spoke and told the maid about the fight she had with Robert. How he slugged her, knocked her out and that she knew what he did while she was unconscious. She swore to her not to say a word about this. Then, the maid helped Emily get ready for bed and gently helped her into bed. Emily again went into shock, her head on the pillow, eyes staring into space. She remained that way until her death. Staring, not saying a word." I sat speechless for a moment." Is that the end of the story?" I asked." Oh, goodness no," replied Henrietta." Although, her personal maid never said anything, it seems that Roberts guilty conscience tormented him. That is very unusual for him since he always thought he was above everything and everyone. The next morning, so they say, Robert was slowly descending the stairs where he met his father who was on his way to breakfast in the dining room. Robert, with a bowed head, sheepishly told his father what had taken place the night before. The captain's face turned beet red, he had a crazed angry look, his eyes narrowed. He then lost control of himself.

He then raised his ebony cane he always used for walking and unmercifully throttled Robert with numerous blows to the head and body. The Butler rushed in to restrain Bartholomew while two servants picked up Robert from the floor. Each one took an arm and helped him to his room. He lay in bed, in and out of consciousness. When conscious, he would mumble wildly. Finally, after two days the captain gave permission to the Butler to call for the doctor."

"The doctor's one-horse buggy pulled up in front of the house. He climbed down and made his way up the steps to the house and was immediately admitted inside by the doorman. The captain was there to meet him and ordered the Butler to take him to Robert's room."

"The doctor entered the room and closed the door. Less than an hour later, he came out of Roberts room and descended the stairs where he met the captain and asked him what had happened to Robert," Henrietta paused." Well again, so they say, Bartholomew told him he had a tremendous fall. That was all he would say about the matter. The doctor told the captain Robert needed to be in the hospital and that he would make the arrangement. Bartholomew opposed the idea vehemently. He said that Robert would be taken care of there. The doctor said he would send for a full-time nurse, again the captain refused the offer, said he will see to Robert's condition. The physician asked if Emily would be his nurse. The captain replied, Emily is indisposed at the present time. The doctor asked if she was alright and should he take a look at her. The captain, whose patience by this time was running out curtly dismissed the doctor."" Well," continued Henrietta." It is said for the next three years both Emily and Robert continued to lie in bed. Emily with eyes open looking at nothing and Robert, just never regained consciousness. The most extraordinary thing is, that almost three years later both Emily and Robert died on exactly the same day, at the same hour. That is the story, Fred."

I asked her how this legend, this story got started." Oh" Henrietta replied, "I imagine gossip between the servants, then to the merchants at the shops on shopping day." "Well. Many thanks to you for your time and information," I said as I rose from my chair to leave. "By the way, is there any mention, of the doll, the one dressed like Emily?" "Well," not so much from the local legend, replied Henrietta." But I think I remember something from the village history, let us see. Henrietta turned the page of the historical volume; her eyes spotted a footnote in exceedingly small print at the bottom of the page." Here is something," she stated." I knew I had remembered something about a doll. It seems Emily and this particular doll were inseparable. They were always seen together. The townsfolk thought this was just the fancy of a rich girl. The last line says, it was rumored that her maid even laid the doll next to Emily while she lay motionless and ultimately passed away." Finished Henrietta." That is very interesting," I stated. " How so"? the woman replied. "Oh, nothing really, just that I thought I heard and seen something peculiar. Did your brother ever mention anything out of the ordinary or something he could not explain?" I asked." Well, like I said his personality changed and he became a nervous wreck, but he never said anything about the house or what went on inside." Thanks again miss Lee, you have been a big help to me," I said as I turned and left.

By this time, it was dusk, so I stopped at the local diner for supper and a large beer. After leaving the diner, while driving home my mind was not thinking of anything of importance. It was now dark; night had fallen and there was a bright full moon. I drove past the edge of town. A couple of miles later, beginning to make the turn into my driveway, I suddenly stopped the car. There, on the second floor of the mansion a light was shining from the window of my upstairs bedroom and what looked like a tiny silhouette looking out. I hurriedly sped up to the front of the house, stopped the car, got out and raced to enter the front door. I sprinted up the two flights of stairs and burst open my bedroom door. The room was dark, no lights on. I flipped the switch on the wall to turn the light on. I scanned the room, my eyes darting from left to right. Nothing seemed amiss. The doll was still sitting on the far chair where I had placed it after the morning encounter I had. I left the room, searched the other rooms convincing myself that I was alone, and everything was secure. It was late and time for bed. After washing up and putting on my nightclothes, I went to my bedroom window. The full moon's light was streaming into the room like a lighthouse beacon. I pulled down the shade about three inches from the windowsill, so that only a small ray of light entered the room. Turning off the light, I climbed into bed. A nice four poster feather bed and fell asleep. It was a strange sort of sleep. Asleep, still vaguely conscious of my surroundings. It was the middle of the night, while in twilight sleep that I felt a slight pressure on my chest. I did not really want to wake up. I forced myself to open my eyes. There, sitting on my chest was the doll, whose face was an inch from my eyes, just staring. This jolted me awake. Instinctively sitting up, using my arm, I batted the doll off my chest and onto the floor. After a few minutes, with my heart pounding and sweating profusely, I managed to get out of bed from the opposite side of where the doll was. I walked around the bed to the door and turned the light on from the wall switch. I hesitantly went over to where the doll was lying and with shaking hand picked it up. It seemed like a normal doll, with its fancy clothes and beautiful painted China face. I was stunned, could not grasp what just happened. Slightly unnerved, I took the thing out of the room and down the hall to one of the other rooms, where I sat it on a chair, went out and locked the door using the key I kept in the keyhole. I went back to my room to try to go back to sleep.

The next morning, after rising, making myself ready for the day, I went downstairs to make breakfast. I went through the library, into the kitchen and started to prepare my meal. Deciding to eat in the dining room, I put everything on a tray and carried it there. The dining room is right next to the library. Like most of the other rooms it is spacious with walls of dark brown oak, polished wooden floors and an overhead chandelier. While eating, I could not stop thinking about what had happened during the night. It did not make sense. I am sure the one beer I had with dinner was not responsible. After finishing breakfast, I put everything back on the tray to take to the kitchen. Going through the library, I just happened to glance at Emily's portrait. I suddenly dropped the tray. Her lips were moving as if she was talking, although there was not a sound to be heard. I turned my head away for a second or two, then looked again. The painting had returned to normal. I went to get a broom and dustpan to clean up the mess on the floor. Depost iting the debris in the waste bin, I left the kitchen, quickly walked through the library and out the front door, got into my car and sped away. I was driving, trying to clear my head, wondering what to do next." Go see miss Lee," I said out loud to myself. Pulling up in front of the historical building, I realized it would not be open for another forty-five minutes. I decided to drive the long stretch of highway to the next town and then back again just to kill some time and think.

Being back in Griegwright and at the Historical Society, I got out of the car climbed the two stairs opened the door and went in to talk to Henrietta." Well, good morning, Fred!" She exclaimed." What brings you back so early in the morning?" "Hi miss Lee," I greeted." Don't be so formal Fred," she replied." Miss Lee-----I mean Henrietta, are you sure there is nothing more you can tell me about the house?"" Maybe something about Emily's portrait or the doll?" "No Fred, that was all. The historical facts and the legend." "Why son, what is the trouble?" "You look like you have seen a ghost," she jokingly said. I hesitated to reply. "You did didn't you," asked Henrietta." Not exactly, I do not think I did," I said. I then related all the incidents that had happened since I acquired the portrait and the doll. After hearing my story, she did not say anything for a few seconds." Fred, would you mind very much if a few friends and I were to visit the house?" "No, I don't mind but why?" I questioned. "I belong to a local psychical society. We like to investigate, if there is something there that needs to be settled or at least brought out into the open so we can discover the meaning behind these events." "I appreciate your offer. I do not put much belief in this stuff but, at this point I will gratefully accept your help miss Lee, I mean Henrietta," I replied. "Good, good," she replied. "What would be a good time for you, Fred?" "The sooner the better." "How does to-morrow sound?" I replied, somewhat relieved." Fine, simply fine. How about we arrive at ten o'clock tomorrow evening? "Asked Henrietta." Thank you so much," said I. I left the building, got into my car and proceeded to drive home.

I had a lot on my mind while on the drive home. Pulling into the driveway, I exited the car. I entered the front door of the house, tossed my keys on the small table in the vestibule and went into the library to go to the kitchen. I did not want to look at the portrait as I passed by but, some irresistible curiosity overwhelmed me. I stopped, turned and looked. The blood froze in my veins. I stood there horrified. Emily was no longer holding the doll. It was on the floor in front of her and it looked like it was painted to resemble walking, walking towards me! I stood transfixed for a moment, noticing the insanely wild expression on the face and eyes filled with hate. It's hand clutching a large knife. I turned, ran out the front door and just stood on the porch for a moment, trying to compose myself and slow down the rapid pounding of my heart. After a moment, I knew I did not want to go back into the house. I needed to do something to occupy my time until I found courage enough to re-enter it. Not wanting to go back into town because that would not accomplish anything. While standing on the veranda looking out, I noticed the flower bed on the other side of the circular drive. I would do some gardening, after all the flower bed had been neglected lately. Walking around to the back of the house and going inside the ground keepers shed, I selected what implements were needed for the job.

Working in the little garden not only killed some time

but was also therapeutic. I was working diligently, concentrating only on the work at hand. After some time, I became tired and quit working for the time being. Standing up, wiping my brow, I turned and looked towards the house. There, at the window on the second floor, my bedroom window, sat the doll just staring at me. I dropped the hand spade I was holding and rushed towards the house. Bounding up the porch stairs and through the front door, I raced upstairs to my bedroom. Turning the knob for the door I quickly opened it. Standing in the doorway, my eyes scanning the room, I could detect nothing out of place, the doll was not there. I began to search everywhere in the room where the thing might hide. Being convinced it was not there, I left my room and walked down the corridor to the room where I had placed the doll the night before. Taking the key from my pocket, I unlocked and opened the door. Without setting foot in the room, I could see the doll was still there but not on the chair where I had placed it, now it was lying on the bed. I immediately shut and relocked the door. Standing there for a moment, trying to comprehend what had just taken place. Turning towards the staircase and while descending it, I was trying to come up with some reasonable explanation for the strange event. Could it be that I worked in the flower bed too long in the hot sun, or might it be a flashback to the night I saw it from the driveway when coming back from dinner. No, -----it had happened all right. The doll did move and all the events I experienced since moving into the house with the portrait and the doll did take place. Going into the kitchen through the library, making a conscious effort not to look towards the painting,

I was going to have an early supper, maybe read a bit, since there was no television or radio, then retire for the evening.

After I finished my light supper, I went to the library, stopping only for a second or two to randomly snatch a book from one of the shelves. I went through the dining room and into the next, which was the living room. This room was spacious just like the others, with a huge oriental style carpet, under which sat a light brown leather couch, two comfortable chairs and two cocktail tables, one on each side of the chairs. I sat in one of the overstuffed chairs and began to read. Not being able to keep my mind focused on the story, troubled by all that had occurred. After a while I decided to go to bed. Although, I did not want to sleep in my room. Grabbing an Afghan cover from the back of the couch, which was on the other side of the room, I made myself comfortable as possible and somehow drifted off to sleep.

In the middle of the night, something, ----a sound had awakened me. Laying there in the darkness, with eyes wide open, I was listening, straining to hear the sound that had disturbed my slumber. There it was again. The sound of swishing, like that of a long dress. A satin gown! It sounded like it was walking in the next room, the dining room pacing back and forth as if trying to decide something. This went on for quite some time and then stopped. Lying there, not wanting to get up and investigate, fearing what I might encounter. I lay there a long time until finally falling back to sleep.

Morning came, I awoke and tossing off the Afghan cover got up from the couch. Making my way through the dining room, library and into the kitchen to make myself some toast and coffee. After eating I went past the library, up the stairs to my room to bathe and change clothes. While changing I decided I would go into town and talk to Henrietta.

As my car pull up to the Historical Society building, Henrietta was just unlocking the door to enter the building." Well Fred, what brings you here this early? Have you had anymore experiences?" Inquired Henrietta." Yes a few let us go in and I will tell you about them." I said anxiously. After entering the building, we sat down at the table we sat at before." All right Fred tell me what happened" she inquired. After I told her about the two latest occurrences, she stood up expressing a look of concern on her face." Whatever is in the house does not want you there. Their actions are becoming boulder and more aggressive," stated Henrietta. "Why? I have not done anything that would initiate any supernatural activity," I replied in a hysterical tone" Just what is the connection to your aunt?" Inquired Henrietta." She is my late mother's sister, "said I." Can you trace your ancestry back far enough to maybe establish a link back to the captain?" She asked. I thought for a moment." Now I remember. When I was a child, my mother used to tell me stories of a great great grandmother and how elegant she was. That she was a prominent figure in the town but hardly ever left the mansion and received only a very few visitors. You want to know something Henrietta? I did not make the connection until now. My great great grandmother's name was Pamela. She had to be the captain's youngest child!" I shouted." Let us not jump to conclusions but, I think you are right. Tonight, we will try to find out what is going on in the house and why," said Henrietta. Relieved somewhat, I bid Henrietta goodbye.

While driving home I was thinking of how I was going to spend the time before the members arrived. Working in the flower bed proved to be a tension reliever before, so that is what I will do now. This time, however, I will work in one of the beds on the side of the mansion, so that I could not look up and see the windows at the front of the house.

While working, I was considering just what I could do to rid myself of the goings on taking place. I came up with three options. One: Move but, Not wanting to do that. After all, the estate had been in my family for generations, and it would not feel right to do that. Two: I could take the portrait and the doll back to Mister Cushing at the antique shop and donate it but, that would not do either. Perhaps someone would buy both because of the connection of the doll being portrayed in the painting. Suppose things continued to happen, frightening and tormenting anyone who owned the pair. I could not live with that. Being the cause of such anguish to others. Three: burn them. Destroy them both. Now, that was an idea that would work. It would solve the problem.

Standing up from what I was doing in the garden, spade in hand, I made my way back towards the gardening shed. Grabbing some rags and pouring a fair amount of gasoline in an old empty coffee can, I went outside to gather small, medium and larger size tree branches and some good-sized logs. I carefully constructed a fire pit. If I do say so myself yeah, it looked like a job of an experienced woodsman, which for a city boy surprised me. Taking a small limb, wrapping the top of it and soaking it in the can containing the gas, I started a bonfire. I raced back to the house, entering it I rapidly went up the stairs to the second-floor room where the doll was, unlocked and opened the door. It was still there. I snatched up the doll from the bed and raced downstairs to remove the portrait from the wall. With a little difficulty I had the picture and took them both outside to the back of the house. The pile of wood was now a blazing inferno. The picture was the first to face the flames, then the doll followed it. It did not take long for the fire to consume them both. After a minute or two making sure my job was a success, I walked back towards the house. Entering the vestibule, I went to the library. What greeted me there was a nightmare come true. There on the wall hung the portrait with the doll sitting on the floor beneath it. I just stood there gazing at the painting, not believing what I was seeing. Turning, then slowly walking as if in a trance, making my way to the living room, I poured myself a drink. I needed both hands to guide the glass to my lips because my hands were shaking so.

I made my way to a chair and sat down." How could such a thing be?" I said out loud to myself. There was nothing to do now except wait. It would be hours before Henrietta and the others would arrive. Sitting in the comfortable chair, my body demanding sleep to recover from the shock and restore my strength, I nodded off.

I awoke in the cool darkness of the room. Looking at my watch, it showed it was almost time for the arrival of the group. The group who would hopefully deliver me from my torment. I did not have long to wait. Three rapid knocks from the front door knocker announced they had arrived. I made my way to the vestibule and opened the door. There stood Henrietta in front of three others. I invited them in." I am so glad to see you all" said I. Stepping inside Henrietta then introduced the others." Fred, may I introduce missis Belasko." (She was a woman in her mid-fifties, five feet tall, slightly rotund, with wire rimmed glasses she had short curly gray hair cut close to the scalp. she was standing next to Henrietta.) "She is a channeler, one who can allow a spirit to enter her body as if it were their own, to make a connection to this world." I extended my hand to welcome her." This is mister Pratt." Henrietta continued. (Standing there smiling was a man in his forties, slender of build, medium height with dark hair combed back.)" How do you do," I said." Mister Pratt is a visual medium," stated Henrietta." He is able to see an entity that might show itself, even though others are unable to see it. "Then there is Chris whom you already know," she said. Taking his hand into my two, I shook it vigorously." Chris is a mental medium. What Pratt can see, Chris can hear, also those that Mister Pratt cannot see."

With the introductions out of the way, I showed them into the living room. After all, had been seated, I offered them some refreshments. All had declined my offer." I know Henrietta had told you some of what is going on here but, there is now more," pausing for a moment I continued and related what had just taken place before their arrival. After I had finished, Henrietta spoke." Fred do not misunderstand this; we must be sure if we are going to help you. Are you sure this really happened, that it was not a vivid dream or a medication you might have taken?" Indignant and taken aback, I led them to the library. Everyone agreed that the doll and the picture were there. We then went outside to the backyard to view what remained of the fire pit.

After going back into the house, we all sat at the long table in the library. Everyone sat in silence, then I spoke.," Henrietta, what is your special gift?"" I can detect vibrations: I can feel what an entity is feeling. The entity can be that of a person in the spiritual realm or inanimate objects, such as buildings, jewelry, clothes, things like that," Henrietta replied." Let us begin our investigation," said Chris." Very well," she agreed. We stood up from our chairs to begin our task." What should I do?" I inquired." You may accompany one of us, but please do not interfere with what we are doing," replied Mister Pratt." Ok let us begin," he said. Our little group splintered off in different directions, agreeing not to investigate the library until the end. Pratt, Cushing and I ascended the staircase to the second floor. We reached the top, took three steps forward and stopped. In front of us was a door." Mr. Carmichael, what is behind that door?" asked Mister Pratt." That is an unused bedroom, now a storage room," was my answer." Let us go in," said Pratt. He opened the door, and we stepped inside. Walking around, Pratt veered off to the left while Chris and I went to the right. Neither Cushing nor Pratt sensed anything. They decided the room was clear of any unworldly presence. Back outside in the hall Chris pointed to the left and asked me what that room was." That is the room where I locked up the doll after it had climbed on my chest."" Let us go in there," ordered Mister Pratt. So, we went inside. Again, Mister Pratt went in one direction, while Chris and I went in the other." I feel as though a spirit was here. It no longer is but, it left all residual trace of its presence. It is hostile, bent on getting even for some wrong done to it. Somehow, I heard its feelings," Chris informed us." I do not see anything," answered Pratt." Fred, can we go to your room now?" asked Chris." Sure, let's go".

Inside my bedroom, the three of us stayed together this time. Mr. Pratt stopped and was looking at the chair against the wall, across from the bed." I see a woman dressed in old fashioned clothes, clutching a doll and weeping, she turned her head, noticed us then disappeared. Chris did you hear anything?" "I heard sounds of crying, words spoken. A word over and over again, Why, why, why? That is all she kept saying." We left the room. And proceeded down to the first floor.

While us men were upstairs investigating, Misses Belasko and Henrietta began their search for answers. They started in the living room. Slowly walking side by side. They were on their guard for any feelings or other psychic phenomenon. They could detect nothing out of the ordinary. The room was clear of any otherworldly presence. Making their way to the dining room, Henrietta immediately received impressions of despair and hopelessness. Her mental state of mind was invaded by feelings of extreme sadness." Misses Balasko I do have to sit down for a moment," Henrietta said." Did you pick up on anything?" asked Misses Belasko." I felt like something wanted to communicate through me but, then it decided not to. I think I picked up on Fred's pacing woman in the satin gown. I must leave this room." Weekly, attempting to rise from the chair, Misses Belasko. assisted Henrietta.

Now, walking through the library, they made their way to the kitchen. Finding nothing out of the ordinary there, they went to wait at the foot of the staircase for the others.

Cushing, Pratt and I were coming down the stairs where we met the two women. We agreed we would go into the dining room to relate our experiences. We were all seated at the table. Chris, Misses Belasko and I sat on one side while Henrietta and Mister Pratt were seated on the other side facing us. Chris was the first to speak. He informed Henrietta and Misses Belasko what we had learned." When we investigated the room where Fred had locked the doll, we felt only the minute sense that something had been there but was not now. I could hear nothing, and Pratt could not see anything. Perhaps Henrietta, you would like to go up later and see what you can discover?" asked Chris." No, that would not be necessary. I am fairly confident it was the psychical Impression left behind by the spirit who periodically inhabits the doll. The spirit is most likely that of Emily. The captain's daughter. Do continue Chris," said Henrietta. He then related what took place in my room. "What we experienced makes me certain that this is not a residual haunting," stated Chris. "Residual haunting, what is that? I questioned." The best way to explain it is to compare it to a videotape that keeps playing the same event over and over again. It is not a spirit or a presence but an impression that keeps manifesting itself. Like I said, this was not that," explained Chris." When I saw the crying woman," Mister

Pratt began," she turned her eyes toward us and looked surprised, that is when she vanished. She knew we were there," concluded Pratt.

Henrietta then related what Misses Belasko and herself experienced." I think the kitchen and the living room are the only safe harbors." "Safe harbors?" Again, I needed a definition." There are places in this house where a living person for some unexplainable reason is not affected by psychic phenomenon," answered Henrietta. Misses Belasko took off her glasses, wiping its lenses with her handkerchief she took from the pocket of her dress." Let us now go into the library," she suggested. We rose from our chairs and exited the dining room.

Entering the library, we sat at the long reading table. Henrietta and Pratt on one side, Chris and I on the other side while Misses Belasko sat at the head." If everyone is in agreement, I would like to see if I can channel whatever is in this house causing these disturbances instead of all of us individually seeking psychic impressions," asked Mrs. B. Everyone nodded their heads in silent agreement. As Misses Belasko sat in silence I spoke. "Should we not hold hands or something?"" That is really not necessary Fred. That is a device used in books and films to create atmosphere. It has nothing to do with generating a force to compel a spirit to manifest itself for communication with the living," stated Henrietta." What we can do is turn down the lights a little, that does seem to have some favorable effect for a positive outcome. Fred, if you would be so kind as to see to the lights we can begin, "asked Henrietta. Misses Belasko then instructed us to turn our eyes toward the picture and the doll." If you would all take a few seconds to look at the portrait, observe the two figures. Make a mental impression in your mind, it will aid us in our attempt to reach out to whatever is here."

Sitting in the semi darkness of the room, all eyes were closed. Mrs. B. then asked us to form an image in our mind of the painting." Concentrate deeply on it make it the only thought you have." After a good five minutes of nothing happening, everyone's looking like wax figures on display, I was about to ask if we should adjourn and try again at a later date. I was on the point of speaking when a voice could be heard, a whisper really, like someone at a distance calling out. The voice seemed to be coming from everywhere in the room. Only one word could be heard. The word why, being repeated over and over again. This continued on for only a few seconds, then nothing more was heard. Moments later, what sounded like the voice of a young woman came from Mrs. Balasko's body.

While the others were still concentrating with their eyes closed, I looked over at Mrs. B. She seemed to be in a trance. Her eyes open in a blank stare, seemingly unaware of what was happening.

"Who are you people, what are you doing in my house!?" Angrily said the voice. The others now with eyes open, focused their attention on Misses Belasko." Leave this house immediately you are not welcome here," demanded the voice. Then Henrietta spoke." Why do not you want us here?" The spirit then materialized standing next to Mrs. Balasko's body. Although visible, the assembled group could see through it. We recognized it as Emily. She was wearing the pink satin gown, like in the painting." Look," I whispered," she is hovering a foot above the floor." The apparition began to move. Gliding behind Mrs. Balasko's body and around the table we could hear the rustling of the gown. The spirit made its way toward me, standing behind me, pointing." What is it you wish to tell us? Why did you go to this man?" Henrietta asked the spirit. Then came a voice emanating from Mrs. Belasko. In the same feminine voice came the angry response." He is a man, a Carmichael. Men are not welcome here. If this one does not leave, dire consequences. First and only warning.". As the spirit slowly vanished, a gasp came fromMrs. Balasko's body, her head hitting the table, she was unconscious. We stood up and rushed to her side. Pratt and Cushing on either side of her, each rubbing and patting her hands while Henrietta rushed into the kitchen to bring back a cool cloth to put on her forehead. Regaining her senses, rising from her chair with the assistance of Mr. Pratt and Chris, she said "That is all for tonight." Noting the time was now one thirty in the morning, we agreed to end the session and go over the encounter the next day. As we were about to leave an agreement was made to meet at the restaurant for breakfast. "Fred, I do not think you should stay here tonight, it is too dangerous. I would like you to stay at my place," invited Chris. "I would normally say no thank you but, I will take you up on your generous invitation." I replied.

At nine o'clock we were sitting in a booth at the restaurant. It was a normal small town eating establishment. Booths with red Naugahyde cushioned seats and backs trimmed with imitation white pine wood. We sat on the window side, tables on the other side split up by an aisle then, a lunch counter separating the kitchen from the eating area. An attractive middle-aged waitress came to our table to take everyone's order.

While, eating the breakfast we had ordered, Mister Pratt wanted to know what the rest of us thought about men not being welcome at the mansion." I know we all grew up hearing the legend of what happened all those years ago, I even told the story to Fred," said Henrietta." So, I think it is quite obvious why there is a hatred of men, especially Carmichael men. After we are finished here, I am going to visit the newspaper office and ask to view their archives, to see if I can find anything about the history of the house and family that might be of interest," Henrietta concluded.

After planning to meet later at Mrs. B's house, the rest of us went about our daily business." Come Fred, let us go to my shop," invited Chris.

Entering through the door and into the antique store, Chris led me behind the counter and through a curtain, which separated the store from the back room. It was a tiny room. There was a small circular dark brown wooden table in of the middle of the room, surrounded by three wooden chairs." Please, sit down Fred," said Chris. After we were both seated, Chris asked me what my thoughts were about what happened last night." Same as the rest of you, I guess" I replied." Would you like a cup of coffee or tea Fred?" Asked Chris." No thanks." "Come Fred help me in the shop, we can look over the items for sale and evaluate their price. It will be a way of killing sometime before we meet the others."

When we were about to leave to go two Mrs. Balasko's

house, Chris had a last-minute customer. After a sale of some insignificant trinket, Chris said to me." This usually happens when I am about to leave. No business all day then I am about to close, and this happens," Chris said with a chuckle. Parking in front of a house with a white picket fence, Chris and I got out of the car. Opening and walking through the gate, we stepped up and stood on a long porch of a typical rural home. A two-story wooden house painted white with green shingles covering the roof. With the knuckles of his hand, Chris knocked on the door. We did not have long to wait. The door opened and there stood Misses Belasko. She welcomed us inside and led us to the living room, which she called the parlor. Mister Pratt and Henrietta were there sitting on the sofa. Misses B. offered us two chairs that were facing Pratt and Henrietta. In between us was a long coffee table. "Now, that we are all here, let me tell you what I found at the newspaper office," began Henrietta. "Looking through the newspaper articles, which were transferred microfiche, I found everything pertaining to the house and the Carmichael family. The earliest was a story about the "Grand House" the captain was building. This was in the year eight-teen-sixty-one. The next few years were about the parties the captain gave for his influential friends. Then it gets interesting. I came across a report about the terrible accident that happened to his only son, Robert," she paused long enough to take a sip of tea. "I could find nothing more for the next five years," she continued. "Then in eight-teen-sixty-six, a double tragedy. Robert had died of his injuries and his eldest daughter Emily had succumbed to a mysterious illness. After that I came across various

articles about accidents and fatalities of men who stayed at
the mansion. It seemed the accidents happened to friends of
Bartholomew or Pamela who were invited to stay for a few
days, celebrating social events or just for a pleasant visit."

"In eight-teen-seventy-one, the paper reported on the
marriage of Pamela, the captain's youngest child. The
wedding reception was held at the mansion, a gala affair.
Afterwards two couples, good friends of Pamela, were invited to spend a few days to enjoy one another's company
and have a relaxing visit," Henrietta paused again, then
continued. "Five days later it was reported that another double tragedy had occurred at the mansion and the husbands
of Pamela's friends had been taken to the hospital." "Now
what I am about to tell you was not in the newspaper. After
reading about the two husbands, it triggered my memory.
A dear friend of mine, whose grandmother worked at the
house during this time, related to her family the events
that happened that night." "It was on the fourth night of
their visit. A fine dinner was served. The men retired to
the living room for coffee and cigars. The women stayed in
the dining room talking. Finally, it was time for bed. The
captain, Pamela and her husband went to their rooms, the
two couples went to theirs, they had adjoining rooms separated by a bathroom. In the early morning hours, terrifying
screams were heard coming from both rooms. The captain,
Pamela, her husband and two servants went rushing towards
the commotion. An identical scene was observed in both
rooms. The wives standing beside the beds, their husbands
in shock, eyes wide open, staring at nothing, mumbling
gibberish. Once in a while the word doll was heard coming

from one of the husbands. After another two days at the house and no sign that the men's condition would improve, they were transported to the mental hospital, located in the next large city, where they stayed for years before they died." "Excuse me, Henrietta," interrupted Mister Pratt. "Is there many more of these articles." "A few but, I have three more things to tell that I think are significant. There was an announcement that Pamela was going to have a baby. The article goes on to report the happiness and excitement of the couple. Five months later, she gave birth to a son. Then, three days later, Pamela 's husband was found dead at the bottom of the stairs.

Like I said, there are a few more articles about accidents and deaths of male friends and relatives but, I think the pattern is clear," stated Henrietta. "Men who are not related in any way to the Carmichael family suffers horrible accidents and the male descendants die." Everyone agreed." What I am about to say next was not found in the newspapers but, what Pamela 's personal maid told my grandmother," continued Henrietta." After returning from the graveside service, Pamela and her maid returned to the house. They went upstairs to check on the baby. As they were about to enter the nursery, they met the nurse maid coming back from investigating the sounds of tiny footsteps running up and down the hall. Entering the room, horrified to see a pillow covering the little one's face, Pamela rushed to the crib, threw off the pillow and held the infant. Luckily, they were in time. The baby was alive. Holding her baby, she noticed the dull sitting at the foot of the crib. It had not been there before."

"Well, what can we do? How do we end this?" I asked." We must formulate a plan of action before we can confront Emily again," said Henrietta matter of factly. "Since the painting and the doll cannot be destroyed," stated Chris." We must somehow put her soul to rest, to persuade her to end her revenge and find peace." "I think the only way that could be accomplished is by a Carmichael," said Misses Belasko. "What if you contact her again, plead with her to show mercy and end this," I asked. "I am afraid that would not do any good," answered Mrs. Belasko." She is right Fred," said Henrietta." What I felt emanating from Emily was pure hatred. The kind so strong, so consuming that it dominated her soul's very existence. It is tying her here. She is unable to find peace and move on until, she feels avenged." Then Mr. Pratt said," now all we have to do is come up with a plan to accomplish this." Mrs. Belasko spoke." We know that whenever there were accidents or death, Emily used the doll to accomplish this. She needed a physical body to do these acts and her spirit entered the doll." "Does anyone have any ideas?" I questioned. Everyone sat silently for a few moments. "Would going to a Catholic priest at Saint Michael's to ask for an exorcism do any good you think?" Chris asked." I do not think it would," answered Mrs. B. "That rite is performed more for banishing a demon than a human spirit but, we will keep the priest in mind, He may be able to help us in another way. Now though, I think we should stop and eat something."

Henrietta and Mrs. Belasko were in the kitchen starting to fix dinner. It was a spacious kitchen, with white as the predominant color and a blue backsplash behind the two sinks and a stove. The light from the midday sun was streaming through the two windows above the sink, with curtains that were tied back." Oh Henrietta, this is so much fun preparing dinner for the others, instead of just for my-self."" Do you have any ideas what we can do to put an end to this?" question Henrietta." Now, no more talk about this. We will have a good dinner and clear our minds. I believe having a fresh start at this will produce a feasible plan," said Mrs. Belasko. She then walked over to the doorway separat-ing the kitchen from the dining room and in a slightly raised voice, so that the men could hear her in the living room, asked them to set the dining room table." You will find ev-erything you need in the China cabinet and no discussing anything about a plan. We need to relax, empty our minds, so we can think more clearly" she said.

Sitting down to a meal of fried chicken, boiled potatoes and green beans, everyone was straining hard to start a con-versation, to initiate some small talk. Finally, in a slightly agitated tone, Mr. Pratt spoke out. "Misses Balasko, I know you meant well, thinking we need to take a fresh look at this problem, and we did need to eat but, none of us can't think of nothing else except, the task that lays before us." All agreed. Henrietta spoke." I was thinking maybe, if we go to where Emily and Robert are buried, take a bit of hair, clip off a piece of clothing from each, making sure to keep the two separated in different containers," she then paused for a moment." Go on" said I." We would then take them over to Saint Michaels and have the priest bless them." "Do you think he will do it?" Asked Chris." I do not see what good that will do," I said. "My thinking is that by doing this and offering another requiem mass over their remains, it might bring peace to Emily and her forgiveness to Robert," answered Henrietta. "We have to try something," said Pratt. "Misses Belasko and I will go to Saint Michael's and see if Father O'Mara is willing to perform the mass and you three men can go to the cemetery to get the bits of cloth and hair," said Henrietta. Chris turned to me. "I am afraid old boy; you will have to spend another night at my place,"

After we finished our meal, while everyone was cleaning up the kitchen, Henrietta called Saint Michael's rectory and asked if the priest would see them to discuss an urgent matter pertaining to saving a lost soul." Thank you, father, let us say in a half an hour?" After hanging up the receiver of the phone, she walked into the kitchen. She informed the others we were expected at the church. Finishing up their work in the kitchen, the women got into Henrietta's car and drove the five miles to the church. The rest of us climbed into Chris's vehicle and made our way to the cemetery. "Let us stop at my place," said Pratt. "We need to pick up the things we will need to take with us to the cemetery." As we were driving, we all sat not saying a word, thinking of what lay ahead of us. Moments later Chris slowed down the car to turn into the driveway and parked in front of Mister Pratts garage. All three of us got out of the car and started walking toward it, with Mister Pratt leading the way. Turning the handle and with an upward motion Pratt lifted the garage door. Going straight to his workbench that was against the back wall of the garage, he quickly found what he was looking for." Here we are!" Exclaimed Pratt, picking up a pair of leather cutting shears." Let us see, we will need a hammer and crowbar." He picked the items off the top of his bench and handed them to me." Now, what can we use for containers?" He absent mindedly said out loud. Walking to the end of the bench, he spied two small jars containing an assortment of used nuts and screws. Emptying the contents on to the bench top, he took an old dry rag and quicky wiped the inside of both jars." I think we have everything we need." Turning around to leave we noticed it was dusk outside." I really think we should wait until it becomes a little darker," I suggested." I think you are right," answered Chris." Well then," said Pratt, "let us go into the house and have a drink."

Meanwhile, at the church rectory, Henrietta and Misses Belasko, were sitting in front of the Priest, who was sitting behind his large, polished mahogany desk. On top of which sat mementos of his life in the priesthood and a picture of his parents. Father O'Mara was a man in his late seventies, solidly built, with short white hair cut close to his head and wearing wired rimmed glasses. His facial expression always gave the impression that he was judging all who asked for guidance. The two ladies would soon find out that appearances can be deceiving.

"How may I help you?"" You said something about rescuing a lost soul," the priest said to them." Yes father," spoke Henrietta." I do not know how you will react to what I am about to ask you." "Please go on" said the priest, In a most reassuring tone of voice." Father, you have been in this parish for almost fifty years so, I am sure in all that time you have heard the legend of the Carmichaels," stated Henrietta." Oh yes, an amusing story," said the priest."

Father, we think---we know that it is more than that, "Misses
Belasko said. Henrietta continued." After my sister-in-law,
misses Lee passed away last month, her nephew, Frederick
Carmichael inherited the house and all its assets." "You see
father." Misses Belasko went on to say. "Frederick's mother
had him out of wedlock, the father left as soon as he found
out she was pregnant. Her mother was a descendant of
Pamela Carmichael. She gave him the Carmichael name and
raised him by herself."" Ladies, this is all remarkably interesting but, please get to the point. I have to visit the hospital
and minister to a couple of the parishioners," said the priest,
anxiously. Henrietta related everything that had happened
to me and what they experienced at the house with the spirit
of Emily. We would like you to say a requiem mass for the
souls of Emily and Robert, tomorrow evening if possible."
"I do not have any problem with that my schedule is clear.
Shall we say six o'clock, "said the priest. "Oh, that would be
just delightful. Could you also bless, some personal items
that belonged to the two?" asked Henrietta. Father O'Mara
answered." Again, I do not see any problem with that."
Rising from his chair, indicating the end of the interview,
all three were on their feet shaking hands.

While the women were at the rectory talking to the
priest, us men were driving down a dark stretch of road in
Chris' late model light blue sedan, leaving the city limits
and traveling the three miles to the cemetery. Reaching our
destination, Chris stopped the car just short of the cemetery
entrance. It was a mostly cloudy night, with a bright crescent
moon peeking out periodically from behind a cloud. Before
us stood an iron fence on both sides of the entrance with a

high iron double door gate, above which, forming an arch, were the words Griegwright cemetery. After a few seconds looking at the foreboding site before us Chris turned the car into the drive passing through the open gate, with only the vehicles running lights to guide us. Slowly, very slowly we made our way following the gravel driveway path. We were straining our eyes, searching for a granite structure, with only the partial moon for assistance. Finally, after what seemed like hours but were only ten minutes, I spotted something." Stop!" I exclaimed in an excited whisper." Everyone look over there, I think I see it." The car stopped, everyone remained in the car for a second or two and then got out. They stood beside the vehicle and tried to see what I was seeing." There about ten yards ahead, on top of that small hill. That looks like a mausoleum," said I." That it does my boy," said Chris. Mister Pratt mentioned skeptically." I think we have a slight problem." "What is that?" I answered." We forgot the flashlights," Mister Pratt said." Now do not panic boys," said Chris, as he was walking toward the rear of the car. He opened the trunk and took out a heavy duty handheld electric lantern." Way to go, Mister Cushing," said Mister Pratt in a joyous tone of voice." Thank you, Mister Pratt, always prepared you know," replied Chris.

The three of us started walking. We were walking side by side with Chris in the middle holding the light. The night was still except for the occasional hoot of an owl in the distance. Walking up hill we finally reached the crypt. We paused for a moment looking at a granite structure. Above the door the word CARMICHAEL was written. All of us stood frozen for a moment. "Supposed it is locked then, what shall we do?" I questioned." Well, if it is, we will have to ask Mister Jenkins, the caretaker to unlock it for us," replied Pratt. "That means going another day living with this nightmare," I said. "Relax Fred we have not even tried to open the door" Chris said.

I looked at the others and reluctantly grasped the handle with both hands, pushed down with all my might. The handle moved downward until an unlocking click was heard. I tried to open the massive metal door but, it was unmovable." Come on, let us all put our shoulders to the door and push," I said. After some minutes there was a slight movement of the door. Stopping to gather more leverage, we tried again. It slowly began to open. The loud and eerie sound of the metal door scraping against the metal door jamb could be heard. Finally, with just enough room to slide past the door, we were inside. The atmosphere hung heavy. It was uncomfortably cool and damp. Not a sound could be heard. It is a lonely and depressing place, giving off a feeling of hopelessness and finality. Standing motionless, Chriss shined the light. First, on the left wall then to the right. "Look, only one person is entombed here. It is your aunt, Fred. All the places where the family members were to be entombed in the walls are empty," observed Mister Pratt. When Chris shined the lanterns beam to the middle of the room, we saw three separate crypts. Moving toward them, our footsteps echoing off the mausoleum walls, we stopped at the first granite enclosed casket. Chris shined the lantern's ray of light upon it. On its top was fastened a small metal plague which read: Emily B. Carmichael---eighteen-forty-eight -----eighteen sixty-six. Chris, setting the lantern on top of the tomb next to us, with the lights ray falling on Emily's resting place said." I suggest we all try to move the lid just enough so we can clip some material and hair." Putting all our combined strength to the task, we were unable to budge the lid. "Fred, try using the crowbar and hammer, that might break the seal," advised Chris. After painstakingly going around the edge of the tomb lid with the hammer striking the crowbar, I felt we could now move the lid. Again, giving it all we had, the cover began to move. "Okay, we just need to slide it over just enough so I can snip off a tiny part of the gown and hair," said Pratt. Continuing our efforts, we managed to pivot the lid over about a foot. Looking down, we viewed the full skull and shoulder of the corpse. Empty eye sockets, a place where there was once a nose and a grimace at the mouth, greeted us. Strands of hair protruded out from underneath the skull. Mister Pratt with shears in hand leaned over the remains then, stopped, turning his head toward us for our reassurance he then continued. He snipped off a few strands of hair then cut off a piece of the gown from the arm of the sleeve. He then handed the items to Chris to put in one of the containers. We all strained to shove the lid back into place. I grabbed the glowing lantern from the top of the crypt behind me. Our dancing shadows on the walls followed us to the next crypt beside us. I pointed the beam of light on the lid of the next stone sarcophagus. The rest walked over to read the inscription on the plaque. Bartholomew T. Carmichael----------Eighteen hundred-----Eighteen-seventy—five. "Not this one," said Chris. Moving on to the next one we read what was on the third.

Robert B. Carmichael Eighteen forty-six----Eighteen-sixty-six. "This is it!" whispered Pratt. Performing the same task to Roberts remains as we did to Emily's; we began our exit out of this house of despair. As we turned to make our way out the light from the lantern went out. We all stopped. None of us could see anything. It is as if all the light in the world was swallowed up. We all stood motionless. Then in the pitch blackness we heard Mister Pratts' voice. "Anyone have an idea of how to proceed?" "I suggest we hold hands, make a human chain and cautiously, step by step follow Chris. Chris, continue on in the same direction you were going before the light went out," I said, trying to sound like I knew what I was talking about. Grabbing the hands of one another we finally reached the entrance to the outside. Even though it was night, it was still brighter than the inside of the mausoleum. We were greeted by wind that was slowly enhancing in its velocity. Mister Pratt and I struggled a little to pull the door closed. "Well, that was quite an adventure," stated Cushing. "I strongly advise you to check your lantern periodically," said Pratt, jokingly.

We all met at Misses Balasko's. "It has been a long and busy night; let us all meet for a late breakfast to discuss our plan of action," said Chris. We all agreed.

The morning sky was overcast. The temperature was cool with the promise of rain in the heavy dark gray clouds. All of us were sitting in a booth at the back of the restaurant, away from the few patrons that were there. The waitress came right away to take our orders. After the waitress had left us, I asked. "What is the plan, what are we doing today?"

"You all seem to already know. Frankly, I am still puzzled." Mister Pratt, Chris and I were sitting across the table from Misses B. and Henrietta. Henrietta spoke. "After Misses Belasko and I returned from seeing the paster, we talked for a while. To let you know, priest is going to say a special mass for the dead at six this evening. Then, immediately afterwards, he will perform a blessing over the items that were Emily's and Roberts. We feel that by taking these to the house with us tonight and contacting Emily, we think we might be able to persuade her to end her vengeance, to forgive Robert and rest in peace." "If you think this is all it takes to end this, why was not this done before? I questioned. "Because no one who owned the house over the years ever asked. It seems they did not want to legitimize the legend and we just could not force them to perform the ritual, now could we," stated Henrietta. "Do you think this will work?" I questioned. "I really do not know?" interjected Misses Belasko, "but we have to try something." The waitress then came to our table with our orders.

After breakfast we all left the restaurant and agreed to meet at Saint Michaels for the six o'clock service. Chris and I went to the antique shop while the rest went about their business for the day, waiting for the appointed time to meet at the church.

We all met at Misses Belasko's. Misses B. was wearing a full-length beige casual dress while, Henrietta had on a violet loose-fitting blouse with a light green printed skirt. Leaving the house, we all got into the car, the ladies in the back and the men in front, with Cushing driving. It was late afternoon, the sky dark and gray, it began to drizzle. Our vehicle pulled into the church parking lot. After I exited the front passenger seat, Henrietta followed from the rear seat with Miss B. closely behind her opening their umbrellas simultaneously. With all of us out of the car and crossing the parking lot, we reached the three steps to the entrance of the house of worship. I held open the tall doors to allow the others to enter first. Inside the church there was a feeling of solemn reverence and holiness. There were Pews on both sides of the aisle leading up to the altar. A large cross hung on the wall looking down upon the altar. A white decorative linen altar cloth covered the top, with two tall candles on either side of the canon, the book of scripture celebrating the mass.

"Let us go to the sacristy, the room behind the altar to see if Father O'Mara is there. It is almost time for the mass to begin," said Henrietta. Entering the room, they found the priest with the two altar servers preparing themselves for the Holy rite. "Excuse me Father", she said. Turning to face them, he greeted the assembled group. "I am ready to start the service, if you all will go back into the church and take your seats, I will begin the service," said the priest. Then Henrietta spoke. "Father, would you set these two items on the altar while you say the mass?" "Of course," he said.

An hour and forty-five minutes later, the mass for the dead completed, the priest said prayers while sprinkling holy water three times over the contents of the open containers. He then crossed the altar, turned and made the sign of the cross. Stepping down from the altar he met with the others.

"Father we would like to make a donation to the church, to help the poor of the parish in Emily Carmichaels name."

"Would you be so kind to bless her donation?" asked Misses Belasko. "Yes, of course," said the priest. "Father, I want to thank you. You have been so accommodating, so understanding, you have our sincere and deepest thanks," I said while shaking his hand.

Leaving the church single file, dipping our fingers in the holy water fount as we exited. We noticed it was raining quite heavily now, as if something had sliced open the rain laden clouds. Standing at the door of the church momentarily, the women opened their umbrellas then, cautiously quick stepped across the parking lot to Chris' car with the men following close behind them with coat collars turned up. Everyone was now inside the vehicle. Chris started it and we were on our way to the mansion. While driving Chris turned on the windshield wipers to high speed. It was still difficult to see the road. The wipers were struggling to keep pace with the rain that was battling the windshield. After riding in silence for ten minutes we finally came to the entrance of the mansion's driveway. I suddenly shouted. "Stop, stop the car, look!" Everyone looked toward the house. There through the heavy downpour and black of the night, we saw the only light emanating from the house. It was on the second floor, coming from my room. There was a tiny silhouette sitting on the sill in the middle of the window. "It has to be the doll. It is as if she is looking right at us," said Mister Pratt. The car was still in gear. Chris took his foot off the brake and the vehicle inched forward, he then pushed slightly against the accelerator, and we continued on up to the front of the house. We sat momentarily. We all exited the car in the same order that we did at the church. We all struggled through the storm to reach the front door. The dark of the night and gale force winds made for a treacherous trek. The women were trying desperately to keep hold of their umbrellas. I rushed up to unlock it. Just as I opened the door, a blinding flash of lightning and a cannon-like sound of thunder ripped through the night sky. We all quickly gathered inside the vestibule. Once inside, the women collapsed their umbrellas and shook the excess water of them. I walked over to the light switch on the wall and turned on the lights. Everyone took off their coats and I hung them to dry in the ante room we were in. "Come, let us go into the dining room, we can relax and compose ourselves," I suggested. "Should not we go upstairs to your room?" asked Henriet "No, that will not be necessary; all we will find is a dark room. In the library we will see the doll sitting on the floor underneath the portrait," I replied to all. Going into the library on our way to the dining room, I flipped the light switch on the library wall that was located on the left, just inside the entrance to the room which turned on all the lights on the first floor. As we entered the room, we all stopped as if on cue. Looking toward the picture, there on the floor sat the doll, just as I said it would be. "Please, this way," I said in a soft tone, extending my arm in the direction of the room. Entering the room, we took a seat at the table. "Can I get you anything.

"Can I make some coffee and bring out some cookies?" I offered. "Yes, some coffee for me," accepted Mister Pratt. "I also," replied Chris. The women declined and took out the water bottles they had put in their purses earlier. Going into the kitchen to make the coffee, the others were strangely silent. Then Misses Belasko spoke to the others." I feel that

I must warn you all of the potential danger we may be about to face." "Danger?" questioned Chris. "Yes. You see, the investigations we have conducted before, were of haunted sites, contacting benign entities, seances to contact loved ones. But this is completely different. There is so much hatred and vengeance that has festered in her spirit that she may be immune to our actions, prayers and rites we perform," She stated. "Well, what can she do to us?" asked Mister Pratt. "She could inhabit our physical bodies whenever she chose to. To make it seem that we act unlike our normal self. She could, I am not saying she would but, that is just some of the dangers we face. She could do so much more," It was at this time that I brought in the coffee. "What did I miss?" I asked. "Misses Belasko was just informing us of what consequences we could possibly expect," said Chris. "Sould we maybe cancel our investigation for tonight," I asked. "I do not think that will be necessary," stated Misses B. "If we know what we could be facing, then we will be armed for whatever comes." "We can assume that Emily knows we are here," stated Mister Pratt. "Before we go into the library to begin, whatever it is we are going to do, -----just what are we going to do?" "I never did know the plan of action?" I questioned. "Misses Belasko and I thought we would make contact with Emily tonight which should not be too hard since we ignored her warning about returning to the house. We would then tell her about the mass that was said for her and Robert, the blessing of their remains and the donation made in her name," said Henrietta. "In other words, plead for mercy and hope she listens to reason," I said. "Exactly," replied Henrietta. I stood up and asked.

"Shall we begin?" Everyone simultaneously rose from our chairs and followed me, single file into the library. Entering through the adjoining doorway, Misses Belasko sat at the head of the long polished wooden table while, the rest of us took our places on either side of it. Each one of us wondering what the night will bring. In the darkened room a loud crack of thunder could be heard from the outside, along with the howling of the gale force wind that seemed to be gaining in intensity. "The storm is becoming worse," said Chris with an anguished look on his face staring at the long narrow curtained windows. I walked over to the small table at the side wall, brought back two good sized candles and sat them in the middle of the table. Chris stood up. Taking a disposable lighter out of his right pants pocket, leaned over the table a little and lit the candles. "Let us begin," ordered Miss Belasko, after an ear-piercing crack of thunder and a bolt of lightning that lit up the entire room for an instant. Again, like the last time, she asked everyone to concentrate exclusively on the portrait of Emily and nothing else. "Concentrate deeply. So thorough that you hear nothing, not even the sound of the storm raging outside. Your mind must be so entuned with Emily," All the while, the roaring of the storm outside was making it difficult for us to give our full attention to the task at hand. Another explosion of cannon like thunder shook the room and the surroundings were lit up the with most extreme flash of lightning. That lasted long enough for us to notice the subject of the picture began to waver. A sign that Emily was about to make an appearance. "I feel her. Her vibrations are getting stronger," said Henrietta.

The rain was hammering unmercifully against the windowpanes spurred on by the extremely high winds. A booming clash of thunder and successive lightning flashes announced that the storm was at its peak. Another thunderous boom, a bolt of lightning and the lights went out. The mansion lost all electric power, with only the light from the two candles to illuminate the room. The shadow from the candlelight is shown upon the portrait. We all observed a thick mist emanating from the object that soon illuminated just the figure of Emily and nothing else that was in the picture. The mist moved toward us and slowly materialized as the image of Emily. She was hovering next to Misses Belasko, as she did before. A slight sound was s heard, a murmur coming from Misses B. "Look, she is in a trance," I whispered. Everyone's attention was now focused on Misses Belasko. As the storm was still raging outside, Emily began to speak through her. In a tone that can only be described an uncontrollable psychotic anger. "You did not heed my warning, now you will all feel my wrath. Then Henrietta spoke to her in a calm and reassuring tone of voice. "Dear, we have come to help you." "I neither need nor want your help," replied Emily angerly. Emily now focused her gaze on Mister Pratt (who was sitting next to Henrietta). The mighty force of her built up rage sent him flying backwards chair and all to slam against the wall. Chris and I rushed over to aid Pratt. While doing this, the doll with great speed flew at me and severely struck me in the face, then dropped to the floor. Stunned and still trying to help Pratt and Cushing Henrietta rushed over to help. She asked Mister Pratt if he was alright. "Yea, I think so," he answered. The three of us

picked up the chair with Pratt still seated and set it right.
Henrietta quickly examined us both. While this was going
on a cluster of books flew off the shelves striking Chris.
Outside with gale force winds and rain pouring, the storm
was still raging with no sign of letting up. We all returned
to our chairs. I was still a little dazed from the blow to my
head from the doll but, able to continue. While Emily was
about to resume with her assault on us Henrietta yelled at
the top of her voice, "Stop—enough!" With another crack
of thunder, a bolt of lightning striking only feet away from
the house, Emilys' attention was now focused on me. On a
table at the far end of the room were writing paper, pens and
a letter opener. In the blink of an eye flew the letter opener
sticking in the back of my chair the point only inches from
my face. Had I not turned my head I would have gotten it
right between the eyes. "I think we should end this session,"
said Henrietta. "Fred, try to bring Misses Belasko out of her
trance but, be gentle, no shaking or shouting. We do not
want to shock her system." As I began to ever so gently pat
the cheek and slightly shake her, she began to come around.
At that moment the image of Emily began to fade. What
happened, did we succeed?" inquired Misses B. "No, we
will have to try again tomorrow," replied Henrietta. The
storm was still raging, I suggested they spend the night.
"Are you serious!" cried Pratt in a highly agitated tone. "I
think we will be safe. We can stay in the servants' quar-
ters," I answered. "Well, it has been quite an evening, and
if the ladies do not mind?" Chris finished while looking
at Misses Belasko and Henrietta. They looked at one another, shrugged their shoulders and Henrietta grabbed one

of the candles off the table, Chris the other. I went over to the small table, opened the drawer and took out two more candles, lit them. I gave one to Mister Pratt and I kept the other. Slowly making our way out of the room to the stairs. Reaching the staircase, we climbed to the second floor, stopping at the top of the landing. I then turned right and walked down the dark hallway, leading our group. The way was dark, lit only by our candles. It was eerie, like I was leading a funeral procession. We passed the room where I kept the doll locked up. We kept walking until we came to a door. "Through here is where the servants lived," said I. "What makes you think we will be unmolested here?" questioned Mister Pratt. "I cannot exactly explain why I feel this way, except that none of the family would ever lower themselves to enter here," I replied. "Not even Emily, who treated everyone as equals?" asked Chris, somewhat confused. "I do not know about that but what I do know is that as a very young child my mom took me to visit my aunt, she stressed to me that, that was a private area, and I was not to enter that part of the house." Opening the door to that wing we proceeded to enter. Walking down the candlelit hall, I stopped. Raising my candle to Choose your rooms; the rooms are still made up but, if anyone would like fresh linen, I can bring some." said I. Looking at the others' faces from the light of their own candles, I could see the trepidation and hesitation they were experiencing. Everyone agreed they would be fine with the rooms as is. They just wanted to retire for the night. Henrietta and Misses Belasko took a room next to one of the bathrooms. Chris, Pratt and I took a room across the hall. The night passed without incident and sleep came quickly.

In the morning, the storm over and power restored, everyone arose from their slumber. We all were going through our morning routine of bathing, teeth cleansing and dressing. We all met in the hallway. "Good morning," I greeted them. Good morning, everyone answered back. "I know we probably did not sleep much but, a good breakfast will bolster our morale," I said. Descending the stairs two by two with myself bringing up the rear, we came to the library entrance. "Misses Belasko and I will make breakfast, you men go to the dining room and set the table," she ordered. I told her I would show her where everything is to be found. "Fred, do you have eggs, bacon, milk butter and coffee?" "Everything but, bacon," I replied. "Okay, we will fix something you all will enjoy, now go," she ordered. While us men were setting up the breakfast table, we were talking among ourselves. "What do you think our next approach will be," I inquired to anyone who will answer. "I for one do not know," stated Chris. "Well, Misses Belasko has a little more knowledge than we do. Although, I do not think she has any more experience in this situation than we do," said Mister Pratt. "What do you mean by that?" I asked. "She has a whole bookshelf of works dealing with psychic phenomenon and its practices but, she has just as much experience as we do since we always work together when investigating an occurrence, we are called in to help. I really cannot figure out our next move," replied Pratt.

Misses Belasko and Henrietta were busily preparing the morning meal. "Henrietta, please pass me a large bowl." After she gave Misses B. the bowl, Henrietta went to the refrigerator and took out a carton of eggs and a jug of milk.

Misses Belasko cracked seven eggs in the bowl and added the appropriate amount of milk and began to vigorously beat the mixture with the whisk she had in her hand. Henrietta went to the pantry and took out a loaf of bread. She then turned on the stove and set a large skillet on the burner and waited for Misses Belasko to soak the bread in the egg solution. When ready Henrietta started to fry the bread. When done to a dark golden brown she reached up to the cupboard and took out a large platter for the French toast. After the coffee was done perking, they found a large tray, setting the food and bottle of syrup on it they walked from the kitchen to the dining room. The table being all set and the men sitting at their places they were ready to dig in. "My, you girls worked a miracle," said Chris with a big smile. "I should say so, considering you had almost nothing to work with," I said with amazement. After Mister Pratt served the women, the men helped themselves. During breakfast we discussed why the offering of the mass, the blessing of her remains had no effect on her. "Maybe she did not know?" I naively said." She knew," Henrietta said. "At one point during the encounter she looked directly at the items." After taking a sip of coffee, Chris said. "Her vengeance is all consuming. She does not want to be at peace. She wants justice, or what she feels is justice." "So, what can we do now?" asked Mister Pratt. "I have been thinking about that. We can hold another séance and try to contact Robert. Perhaps if we bring the two together, we can somehow resolve the bitterness she feels towards him and for all men," replied Henrietta. "Do you think this will do any good Misses Belasko?" she continued. "It may, frankly I do not know what else to try," she replied.

"Well, if everyone is finished with their meal, you men can start clearing the table, Misses Belasko and I will clean up the kitchen," Henrietta instructed. After everyone had quickly completed their tasks, we all assembled in the living room, Misses Belasko asked if everyone was ready to go back to the library to begin the séance. It is late morning; does not this have to be done at night?" I questioned quizzically. "To the entities in the spirit world there is no day or night as we know it. No special time that they can enter our realm," said Misses Belasko. We all rose from our chairs and in a single file walked through the dining room and into the library. All of us were headed towards our chairs. When reaching my chair, I was about to sit down when Misses Belasko asked me to draw the curtains and light the candles. "Fred, this is not for the spirits, it is more for us, so that we can see more clearly any entities that might manifest themselves." Sitting around the table, the darkened room lit only by two candles and the mid-morning sun peeking through the sides of the drapes, we were ready to begin. "Again, we should all deeply concentrate, thinking only of Robert. Mentally drawing him to us," instructing Misses Belasko.

Misses Belasko with eyes closed and focusing solely on Robert and nothing else asked to speak to Robert. "We wish to commune with the spirit of Robert Carmichael. We know you must be in perpetual torment, and we wish to help you. Please, come and join us. We wish to put your soul to rest," pleaded Misses Belasko. "We beseech you Robert Carmichael to communicate with us, to let us help you to find peace. To reconcile with your sister Emily." All was still for a moment. Then the flames of the two candles flickered slightly but that was all that occurred. Then for thirty minutes nothing more happened. I was about to speak when Chris spoke. "I hear a mumbling, a masculine voice." "Does anyone else hear it?" None of us did. "It is becoming more pronounced," he said. "I am beginning to see a mist emanating from the mantle over the fireplace," said Mister Pratt. The mist was clinging to the photo of the captain. "Who is with us?" inquired Misses B. There was no reply. Again, with a little more urgency in her inquiry, she asked the question. "Who is here?" A voice answered. "I am Bartholomew Carmichael." "Why have you come to us?" Misses Belasko questioned. To end this," the spirit answered. "Where is your son?" asked Henrietta. Mister Pratt spoke. "I am beginning to see a form materializing." A few moments later the rest of us saw the visage of the captain. He was a large figure, tall, wearing the dress uniform and cap of the merchant sailing vessel he commanded. He had a full beard, glasses and longish curly grayish hair. "My son is in everlasting torment, trapped in his own guilt." "How can you end this?" "How can you bring peace to this house and your descendants?" Henrietta wanted to know. All was silent for a few moments. "Again, I ask you captain Carmichael, how can you end this?" "Summon the poor soul of my daughter Emily," he replied.

In the semi-darkened room, eyes closed, our thoughts now focused on Emily. While sitting there in anxious anticipation, a sound was heard coming from the direction of the portrait but, it did not come from the picture, it came from the doll sitting underneath it on the floor. It stood up on its tiny feet, turned and began to run in the opposite direction of our assembled group. "Stop!" shouted the captain in his commanding voice. At that moment the doll immediately dropped to the floor. Covering the doll, we could see a misty cloud rising from it and drifting toward Misses Belasko. The mist slowly dissipated, and the figure of Emily appeared at her side. Looking across her over to her father, the two were face to face. "Ooohh, Papa." The tone of Emilys voice was pleading and pitifully heart breaking, as if she was seeking comfort and succor from her father. Reaching out his hand the captain spoke. "My dear, dear daughter, come with me now. We can both be with Pamala enjoying everlasting peace and joy together." Then, the apparition wavered and became covered in a dark pink transparent shroud. She then spoke. The tone of Emilys;' voice became bitter and indignant, rising in pitch as she spoke. "You want me to forget what happened. To know I could have married a loving husband, had children, wealth, social standing? I would have had a bright future but, that was all taken away from me. I shall never rest until; I can archive full satisfaction." "My dear, you will never find peace and be at rest if you cannot forgive and move on," spoke the captain in a fatherly tone of voice. After a slight pause, I looked past the shade of Emily and saw a transparent figure of a man walking into the library from the vestibule. It did not start out as a mist like the rest but was a complete apparition. He was dressed in a cut-a-way tux suit. It was all tattered and torn with worms crawling up and down the dried earth covered suit. His face was pot marked. He had boils covering his face and his mostly bald pate had some strands of thin hair. Everyone noticed me and followed my gaze. There, standing behind Misses Belasko, between Emily and the captain was this man staring blankly. "Who are you?" asked Henrietta directly. "I am Robert Carmichael," he replied in an otherworldly monotone voice. "Leave!" shouted Emily in a tone filled with hatred and rage. A slight wind could be noticed filling the room.

"Sister, I come to beg, to plead with you to find it in your heart to forgive the awful wrong I did to you. Not to release me from my torment but, to give pardon to the others that may come along." The wind in the room was steadily increasing in intensity. "I shall not in any way give the slightest comfort to you," she screamed. "I seek not comfort for myself but, for you," he said emotionally. "If you can truly pardon me for the despicable way I treated you, there is a way to make things right." Now, Robert had everyone's attention. "In my utter and eternal despair and loneliness, the Lord, in all his consuming wisdom and mercy, appeared to this undeserving wretch." As Robert was speaking the wind dissipated. "The Lord asked if I genuinely wanted to right the wrong, I did. I answered humbly that there would be nothing else I would ever want." A look of doubt was on Emilys face." And why would he single you: of all beings to grant this gift?" "He said that he would welcome you to join the entities of those who would have been your husband and your four children, had you lived. The man who was destined to be your husband died young in a boating accident. The souls of your unborn children are waiting to meet their mother." "You did not answer my question. "He knows you have suffered enough anguish and heart break. Your actions are forgiven and all those you have harmed are now residing in paradise. You can exist in eternal joy and happiness, but you must be truly and without deception. forgive me and all others you think must suffer your wrath." "How can I be forgiven for causing death and physical and mental pain?" They were destined to leave this plane of existence at that time, and you were the instrument to accomplish this." " Sooo----I am to release you from your hell and let you be at peace?" Emily asked with great annoyance and ill temper. "No sister, if you accept this most gracious and generous gift from our creator, the payment would be that my torment, loneliness and despair, would be doubly enhanced without any chance of deliverance, "he informed her. All was quiet for a moment. "You would do this for me?" asked Emily in a subdued and solemn tone of voice. Her mood softened. With a look of concerned compassion, she spoke again. "Dear brother, your sacrifice for me and your unselfish act to right this unforgivable wrong has brought heartfelt compassion and forgiveness from me. I most readily accept this blessing of the Lord."

His apparition was about to fade away when Emily called out to him. "Robert! I will receive this undeserved gift but, only if the almighty will grant you the forgiveness and peace that I have truly shown you, if not I cannot rest, and my vengeance will continue. I say this not as a threat but, to show my deepest gratitude to you for my salvation." Then, the darkened room was filled with a radiant light. The brightness so blinding we had to shade our eyes by putting our hands above our eyebrows. The atmosphere there was engulfed in a feeling of peace that would be hard to explain to others. Henrietta looked over to Misses Belasko who was still in a trance state. I glanced at Chris and Mister Pratt who sat looking at me.

The manifestations of the captain, Emily and Robert began to slowly merge together, forming an incandescent ball of light, emitting a great brilliance. Then again, shielding our gaze from the blinding light, the essences of the three spirits began gradually fade away. They were gone. The room was once again in the semi darkness it had been at the start of the séance with the two candles still burning now, much shorter than before. We were waiting for Misses Belasko to come out of her trance. Henrietta took her hand and began tapping the back of Misses B, s wrist gently until she came out of it. Asking for a drink of water, I stood up and went to the kitchen to take a glass from the cupboard and filled it with water. Taking it to Misses Belasko Henrietta took the glass because Misses B.s hand was to week to grasp the glass. Raising the glass to her lips, with a slight upward motion, she took a took a couple of swallows. We all sat in silence for a moment. "Is that it, is the curse ended?" I asked in a subdued but excited voice. Then Henrietta spoke. "Yes Fred, I think I can safely say that it is over. Emily has found peace." We all stood up from our chairs and moved away from the table. We were walking towards the living room. As I was walking, I suddenly felt my foot step on something then, I heard a crack. Stepping back, we all looked down. I had stepped on the doll and crushed it. Looking at the rest, Henrietta stooped down and picked it up. With a horrified expression shown on my face, I asked Misses Belasko if that would have any negative effect on our outcome. With a chuckle she said "Relax Fred. Now that is just an antique doll although, you probably could have gotten maybe five thousand dollars for it at auction." "I am afraid it is in too bad of condition to be fixed," said Henrietta. "That is oh kay, I just want to be rid of it," I replied. "Let us have a drink and make a toast to Emily", said I. I went to the sideboard and put five small wine glasses on a tray then filled them with sherry I went around to everyone, each took a glass. Standing in solemn silence, I raised my glass, and the others did the same. "Here is to Emily, may she always be at peace and to the house of Carmichael." In unison all replied "Here, Hear". After our toast we threw our glasses into the fireplace, as is the custom.

"Well Fred, I hope we are not going to lose you? It would be nice if you could settle here," asked Chriss. "Yes, we all would like that," said Henrietta. "I like it here, this is my home now," I told them. "Fred, I would like the portrait of Emily if you do not mind," asked Henrietta. "Sure but, why." "I cannot really say. Maybe it is to commemorate our work here or to remind me of my brother or both," she stated. "Sure, I would be more than happy to give it. After all it was you who gathered everyone together to help me."

"Well then let us have dinner," invited Mister Pratt. As we all left for town, I was secure in the fact that I would return to a normal and peaceful home.

Printed in the United States
by Baker & Taylor Publisher Services